Beowulf

Written by Anita Ganeri   Illustrated by James Ives

Collins

Long ago, King Hrothgar was king of Denmark. He built
a huge hall, called Heorot, on top of a hill. Heorot was
built from the finest wood and decorated with the most
splendid gold.

Every night, the king invited his warriors to Heorot for
a great feast. There was always plenty to eat and drink.
Late into the night, the king and his men sang and laughed,
and ate and drank until they fell asleep.

Outside the hall lay a stinking swamp. It was home
to a dreadful monster, called Grendel. The noise
from the hall woke Grendel up. It made him
angry – he hated the sound of laughter.

4

Grendel marched to Heorot and smashed open the doors. Roaring with rage, he attacked many of the king's warriors. Night after night, Grendel came back until no one dared to stay in the hall any more.

A brave, young warrior from Sweden heard about King Hrothgar's troubles and set off to help him. His name was Beowulf.

"I have come to kill the monster," Beowulf told the king.

The king shook his head sadly.

"Many men have tried," he said.
"And all of them are dead."

But Beowulf was not frightened of Grendel. He and his men spent the night in Heorot, waiting for the monster to come. All around him, his warriors fell asleep. But Beowulf was only pretending …

Before long, Grendel stormed into the hall and began to attack Beowulf's men, one by one. Quickly, Beowulf jumped to his feet and grabbed hold of the monster's arm.

With all his might, Grendel struggled to get free – but Beowulf would not let go. Grendel thrashed and crashed around, making the hall shudder and shake. Still Beowulf held on. Then, with a mighty yell, Beowulf tore off Grendel's arm!

Grendel howled with pain. Then he staggered back to the swamp to die.

King Hrothgar was delighted and held a great feast in Heorot to celebrate. But his happiness did not last for long ...

That night, the hall was attacked again, but this time, the monster was Grendel's mother. She wanted revenge for her son's death. In front of the king, she killed Leofric, his bravest warrior.

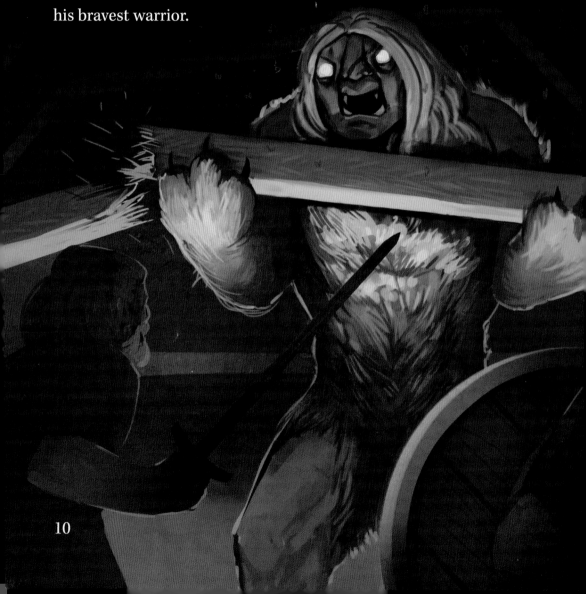

"Beowulf! Come quickly," shouted King Hrothgar.
"Grendel's mother is more dangerous than her son.
If you can't help us, we're doomed!"

Beowulf tracked the monster down to her home – the bottom of a deep, dark lake. It was a terrifying place. Beowulf looked long and hard at the murky water. Then, picking up his trusty sword, he dived into the lake.

Suddenly, Beowulf felt something grab his leg.
Grendel's mother had been waiting for him.
She dragged him deeper and deeper into the dark water
until they reached a huge, underwater cave, filled with bones.

13

Grendel's mother gripped Beowulf even tighter.

"You killed my son," she hissed. "Now I shall kill you!"

Beowulf lashed out with his sword. Again and again he tried, but the sword couldn't hurt Grendel's mother.

Nearby, Beowulf saw a pile of treasure that the monster had stolen. On top lay a gleaming sword. He could see it looked better than his own sword. Quick as a flash, Beowulf grabbed the sword and cut off the monster's head. Then he swam back to dry land and gave the head to King Hrothgar as a prize.

Beowulf went home to Sweden, a hero, and became king.
He ruled wisely for 50 years. But now he was old and tired
of fighting. Until, one day …

News came of a terrible dragon flying over the villages
and fields of his land. It breathed fire and burnt everything
in sight. A thief had stolen a cup from its treasure and
the dragon wanted revenge. People were terrified and begged
the king for help.

Gathering his warriors, Beowulf rode out to the dragon's den.

"Stay here," he told them. "I shall fight the dragon alone."

The battle was fast and fierce. Beowulf lunged at the dragon
with his sword but it was too quick for him. It sank its teeth
into Beowulf's neck and he slumped to the ground.

A warrior, called Wiglaf, came to help the king.

Wiglaf stabbed the dragon and it fell down dead.

But it was too late for Beowulf.

Then Beowulf, great hero and killer of monsters, closed his eyes and died.

His warriors carried his body to a cliff overlooking the sea. Then they laid his body on a pile of wood and lit the fire. Afterwards, they buried his ashes under a great pile of earth alongside the dragon's treasure.

21

Being Beowulf

strength

cleverness

speed

bravery

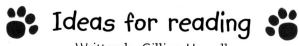

Ideas for reading

Written by Gillian Howell
Primary Literacy Consultant

Reading objectives:
- draw on what they already know
- predict what might happen on the basis of what has been read so far
- continue to apply phonic knowledge and skills as the route to decode words
- make inferences on the basis of what is being said and done

Spoken language objectives:
- use relevant strategies to build their vocabulary
- articulate and justify answers, arguments and opinions
- give well-structured descriptions, explanations and narratives for different purposes
- maintain attention and participate actively in collaborative conversations

Curriculum links: Citizenship; History

Interest words: Hrothgar, Heorot, dreadful, laughter, Beowulf, delighted, Leofric, fierce

Resources: pens, paper, collage materials

Word count: 763

Build a context for reading

- Look at the cover illustration and read the title together. Ask the children if they have heard the story of Beowulf. If any have, ask them to say what they know about it. If they are not familiar with it, ask them to say, based on the cover illustration, what sort of story they think it will be.

- Turn to the back cover and read the blurb together to confirm the children's ideas about the story. Discuss what sort of character they think Beowulf will be.

- Explain that the story comes from an ancient Scandinavian poem and uses some names which may be unfamiliar to them. Ask the children to turn to p2 and point out the word *Hrothgar*. Ask them how they think it should sound, and explain that the *h* is dropped to sound like *rothgar*, with the stress on the first syllable. Tell them they will need to use their knowledge of sounds to work out other new and unusual names in the story.

Understand and apply reading strategies

- Ask the children to read up to the end of p15, quietly. Listen in as they read and prompt as necessary. Ask them to think about what sort of characters both Grendel and Beowulf are and make notes of words used in the book to support their ideas.

- Pause at the end of p15 and ask the children to discuss what they think will happen to Beowulf after he gives the head to King Hrothgar.